THE USBORNE
FIRST BOOK OF THE
PIANO

John C. Miles

Edited by Judy Tatchell

Designed and illustrated by Kim Blundell

Consultant: Barrie Carson Turner
Original music and arrangements by Barrie Carson Turner

Contents

About this book

This book is about learning to play the piano. It explains how the piano works and shows you how to read music and play tunes.

You will probably have heard many of the tunes in this book already. This can make it easier to play them. Others have been specially written.

As soon as you have learned the first few notes on the piano, there are tunes for you to play. Each time you learn something new, there is a tune to help you practice it.

How big was the biggest grand piano? When was the first piano made? You can find out answers to questions such as these in the book. There are also puzzles for you to try, with answers at the end.

For the first tunes, you only need to use one hand at a time. As you get better at playing the piano, you can start to use both hands together. This makes piano playing more interesting.

You can find a whole section full of tunes to play near the end of the book. There are tunes from classical music, Christmas carols, folk songs and duets (tunes for two players).

Getting ready to play

Before you start playing, you can find out about the piano and how it works on these pages.

Violin bow

The first piano

The first piano was made in about 1710 by an Italian called Cristofori.

How the piano works

The piano has lots of strings inside. When you play the piano, little hammers hit the strings. These make the sounds.

Some other instruments use strings. You pluck the strings on a guitar and a harp. On a violin, you draw a bow across the strings.

Inside your piano

Ask someone to open your piano. Stand on a chair so that you can see the strings and hammers. What happens when you press a black or white key?

Press gently and you make a soft sound. This is because the hammer hits the string gently.

Press firmly and you make a loud sound. This is because the hammer hits the string hard.

If you take your finger off a key the sound stops. What happens if you leave your finger on a key?

You put your music on the music stand.

The first name for the piano was pianoforte. In Italian, *piano* means soft and *forte* means loud. A piano can make both soft and loud sounds.

The section with all the black and white keys is called the keyboard. Each key is attached to a hammer inside the piano.

Strings

Hammers

These are called keys.

These are called pedals. They affect the sound that the piano makes. You don't need to use them for the tunes in this book.

Different sorts of piano

There are three main types of piano.

This is an upright piano. It is small enough to fit into any main room in the house. It is called an upright piano because the strings inside are upright.

Grand piano

Grand pianos are bigger. The strings inside are stretched out flat. Grand pianos are usually used for concerts. They can make a louder sound.

An electric piano does not have strings. It needs a supply of electricity to make sounds. You must plug it in and switch it on before you can play.

Sitting at your piano

Try to relax before you start to play. Sit on the piano stool and put this book on the music stand.

Your fingers should be slightly curved.

You need to be able to reach the keys easily without stretching.

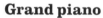

Your back should be straight.

Hold your elbows slightly away from the sides of your body.

You can usually raise or lower the piano stool until it is at the right height for you.

The stool is too high.

The stool is too low.

The stool is just right.

The part of your arm between your elbows and wrists should be flat.

An amazing piano

This was an early attempt to make an upright piano.

This strange piano is called a Giraffe piano, made in about 1825.

Musical sounds

Music is made from lots of sounds, called notes, all put together. On this page and the next, you can find out about the different sorts of notes you can play on your piano.

At your keyboard

Low sounds

On the piano you can make high notes by pressing the keys on your right. You can make low notes by pressing the keys on your left.

High sounds

Left. Lower down the piano.

The further away from you on your left, the lower the notes sound.

The further away from you on your right, the higher the notes sound.

Right. Higher up the piano.

Play some high and some low notes. Use both the black and the white keys. Where are the highest and the lowest notes you can play?

High and low sounds

In music, there is a word for how high or low a note sounds. This is called its pitch. The higher a note sounds, the higher its pitch.

6

Letter names of notes

When you write, you use letters of the alphabet to spell out words. In music, you use the first seven letters of the alphabet to spell out tunes.

The picture below shows part of the keyboard. Each key has a letter name. The note names go from A to G. Then they start again from A.

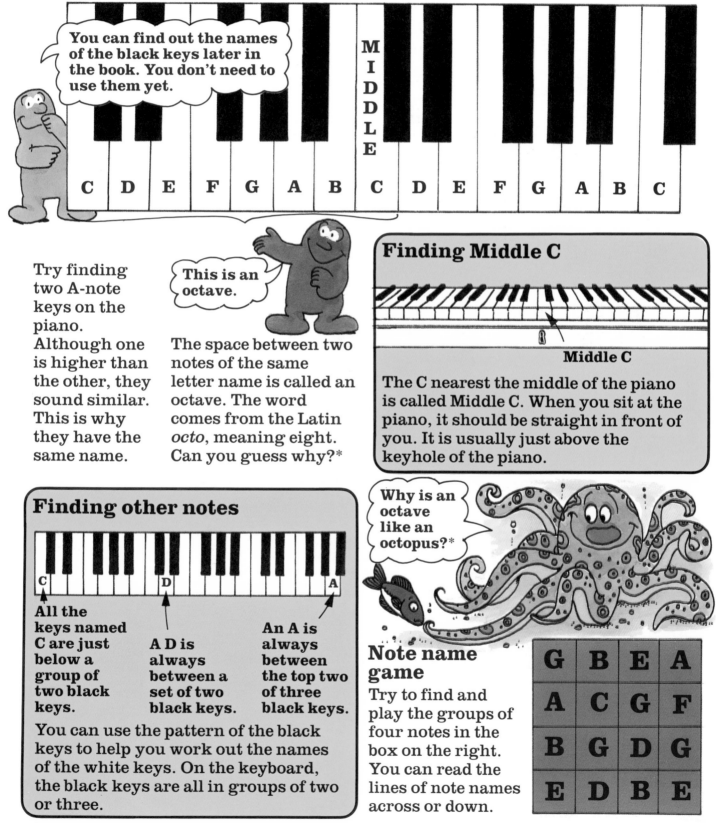

You can find out the names of the black keys later in the book. You don't need to use them yet.

C D E F G A B C D E F G A B C

MIDDLE

This is an octave.

Try finding two A-note keys on the piano. Although one is higher than the other, they sound similar. This is why they have the same name.

The space between two notes of the same letter name is called an octave. The word comes from the Latin *octo*, meaning eight. Can you guess why?*

Finding Middle C

Middle C

The C nearest the middle of the piano is called Middle C. When you sit at the piano, it should be straight in front of you. It is usually just above the keyhole of the piano.

Finding other notes

C D A

All the keys named C are just below a group of two black keys.

A D is always between a set of two black keys.

An A is always between the top two of three black keys.

You can use the pattern of the black keys to help you work out the names of the white keys. On the keyboard, the black keys are all in groups of two or three.

Why is an octave like an octopus?*

Note name game

Try to find and play the groups of four notes in the box on the right. You can read the lines of note names across or down.

G	B	E	A
A	C	G	F
B	G	D	G
E	D	B	E

* Answers on page 63.

Writing music down

On these two pages you can begin to find out how to read music. This means that you can play tunes that other people have made up and written down. You will even be able to write down tunes that you make up yourself.

Piano music

Piano music is written on two sets of lines called staffs. Each staff has five lines. The top staff is for the notes above Middle C. The bottom staff is for the notes below Middle C.

Usually, the right hand plays the music on the top staff and the left hand plays the music on the bottom staff.

The bracket shows that both staffs are to be played together.

There are no notes on the staffs yet. They are a bit like blank sheets of paper with no words on them.

This is a treble clef. Treble means high. For instance, a boy's voice is called a treble voice.

This is a bass clef. Bass means low. A bass singer sings low.

Top staff

Bottom staff

You can tell the staffs apart because of the signs at the beginning of them.

The top staff always starts with a sign called a treble clef.

The bottom staff always starts with a sign called a bass clef.

Putting notes on the staff

Each note on the piano except Middle C has its own line or space on the top or bottom staff. Middle C has its own extra line in between the two staffs.

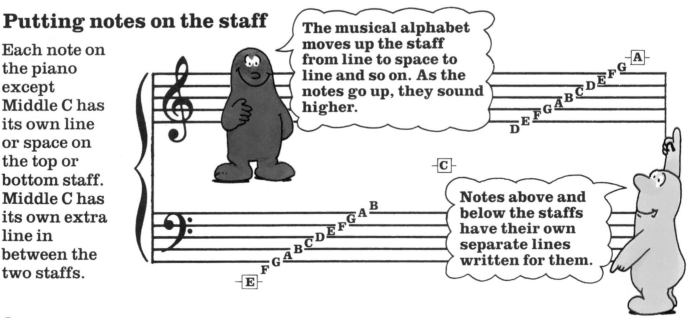

The musical alphabet moves up the staff from line to space to line and so on. As the notes go up, they sound higher.

Notes above and below the staffs have their own separate lines written for them.

Reading the notes

Find and play Middle C. Then, moving up the top staff, find and play the notes on the lines above Middle C.

The keyboard picture on the right may help you to remember the names of the keys.

Then find and play the notes in the spaces on the top staff.

On the bottom staff, see if you can find and play the notes on the lines. Start from Middle C and work down. Then do the same for the spaces.

As the notes move up the staff, they move to the right of the piano and sound higher.

As the notes move down the staff, they move to the left of the piano and sound lower.

A memory trick

Here is a way to help you learn the names of lines and spaces. Just remember this sentence — Good Birds Don't Feed Any Cool Elephants.

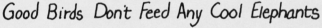

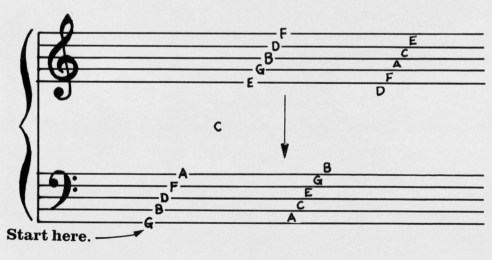

Say each word of the sentence as you point to a line on the staff. Start with the bottom line and work up.

When you get to the top line of the top staff, go back to the bottom space on the bottom staff. Carry on saying the sentence as you go up all the spaces.

What is rhythm?

A rhythm is a pattern of long and short sounds. The pictures on the right show some simple rhythms.

Your heartbeat

Horse's hooves

Beating of a drum

Clock ticking

Clapping rhythms

Try clapping the rhythms below. Say the words and clap as you say them.

March-ing, march-ing, left, right, left, right
(clap clap clap clap clap clap clap clap)
March-ing down the dust-y road
(clap clap clap clap clap clap clap)

Light - ning   ne-ver strikes
(clap - clap clap - clap clap)
In   the   same place twice
(clap-clap   clap clap clap)

The rhythm above is the simplest kind of rhythm. All the sounds are the same length.

CLAPS SLOW QUICK ||||

In this rhythm, some claps are slow and some are quick. For instance, "Lightning never" has four quick claps.

Counting rhythms

Every song or tune has a rhythm. When you are playing tunes, you cannot clap at the same time. Instead, you can count to keep the rhythm steady.

Try the simple counting rhythms below. Say the words, and listen as you say them. Can you hear how the rhythms are different?

This rhythm sounds like a steady march.

One, two   one, two
one, two   one, two

This rhythm has a gentle swing to it.

One, two, three
one, two, three

Here is another steady rhythm.

One, two, three, four
one, two, three, four

It helps to say "one" louder than the other numbers.

A one-count note

When you write music down, different note shapes tell you which sounds are long and which sounds are short.

This type of note is called a quarter note. This is one of the commonest notes. It lasts for one count.*

Here is one of the counting rhythms from the previous page. There is one quarter note for each count. Can you see how the quarter notes fit the rhythm?

| 1 | 2 | 3 | 4 | 1 | 2 | 3 | 4 |
| clap | clap | clap | clap | clap | clap | clap | clap |

Note name reminder

Letter name of note = pitch of note (how high or low it is.) — Note B

Rhythm name of note = how long or short it is. — Quarter note (one count)

Writing rhythms down

When music is written down on a staff, the counts are divided into groups. Each group is called a bar.

The numbers at the beginning of a tune show how many counts there are in each bar. These numbers are called the time signature of the music.

In the tune on the right, there are four quarter note counts in each bar.

The top number four tells you how many counts there are in each bar.

Bar

Bars are separated by a bar line.

The bottom number four stands for quarter notes.

Where the notes are written on the staff tells you which notes to play. For instance, a quarter note here tells you to play the note E.

In arithmetic, you write 1/4 with the four on the bottom. This may help you to remember that a four on the bottom of a time signature stands for quarter notes.

More time signatures

The time signature on the right tells you that there are three quarter note counts in each bar.

Can you figure out what the time signature should be for this piece of music? (Answer on page 63).

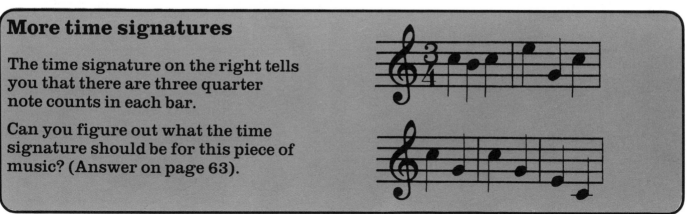

* The note is called a quarter note because it lasts for one quarter of the length of a whole note. See pages 16 and 63.

First tunes

Here are some tunes for you to try. They use quarter notes and the time signatures you found out about on the last two pages.

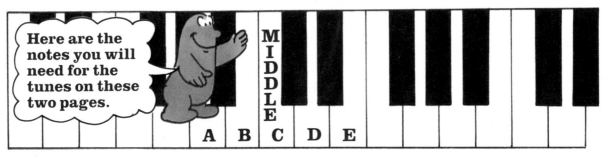

Your first tune

Here is a tune in $\frac{4}{4}$ time. You can use any finger of your right hand to play it. It will help to keep the rhythm steady if you count a slow four before you begin. Then keep counting quietly to yourself as you play.

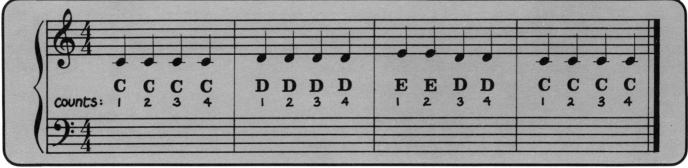

A $\frac{3}{4}$ tune

This time signature shows that there are three quarter note counts to a bar.

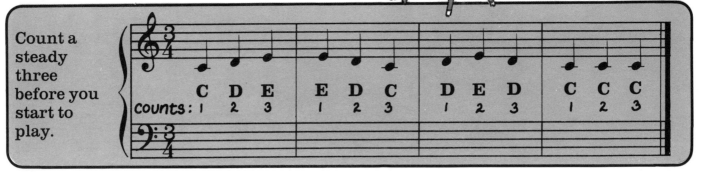

A $\frac{2}{4}$ tune

This tune is a march. It has two counts in each bar.

$\frac{2}{4}$ is like $\frac{4}{4}$ cut in half.

counts:

C	D	C	D	E	D	D	C
1	2	1	2	1	2	1	2

Left-hand tunes

Now try playing this tune with your left hand. Just as the first tune you played went up from Middle C, so this tune goes down from Middle C.

C B A B   C B A B   C B A B   C B C C

When Middle C is to be played by the left hand, it is written close to the bottom staff. When it should be played by the right hand, it is written close to the top staff.

right hand
left hand

When notes are written above the middle line in either staff, their tails go down. Below the middle line, their tails go up.

Here is a tune for the left hand in $\frac{3}{4}$ time.

C C B   A A B   C C B   C C C

13

Using different fingers

Here you can find out how to play the notes in a tune more smoothly. As you get better at playing the piano, it will also help you to play notes more quickly.

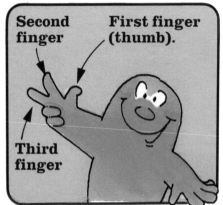

Second finger

Second finger   First finger (thumb).

Third finger

Start to press the next note down as you are lifting your finger from the one before.

Coming up.

Going down.

Play these three notes one after the other. Use your second finger only. You have to take your finger off each note before you can play the next one.

Now play the same three notes again, using your thumb for Middle C, your second finger for the second note and your third finger for the third note.

Press the next note before you have finished taking your finger off the one before. Can you hear how this makes the music sound smoother?

Finger numbers

The tunes in this book tell you which finger to use to play a note. Each tune has numbers in it near the notes. These numbers tell you which fingers to use.

The picture below shows you which number stands for which finger.

Every finger has a number.

This is why ducks cannot play the piano!

Remembering the numbers

Hold both your hands in front of you, palms together. The fingers which touch each other have the same number.

The little finger on each hand is number 5.

The thumb on each hand is number 1.

At the piano

Now put your hands on the keyboard, with both your thumbs on Middle C. Play C, D, E, F and G with fingers 1, 2, 3, 4 and 5 of your right hand. Then play C, B, A, G and F with fingers 1, 2, 3, 4 and 5 of your left hand.

When you play fingers 1 to 5 of your right hand, the notes get higher. When you play fingers 1 to 5 of your left hand, the notes get lower.

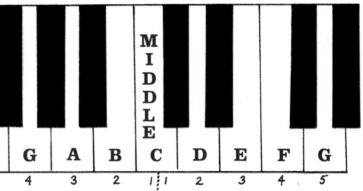

Try playing the notes below. Start with the little finger of your left hand (number 5) on note F. Now move up the piano playing one note with each finger.

Don't forget to play Middle C twice – once with your left-hand thumb and once with your right-hand thumb.

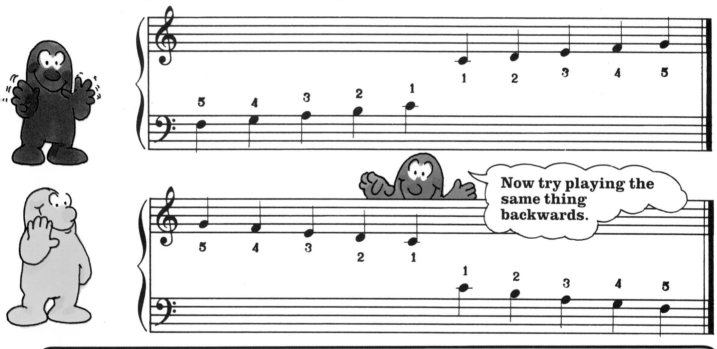

Now try playing the same thing backwards.

A tune with finger numbers

Here is a tune to play. The numbers tell you which finger to use for each note.

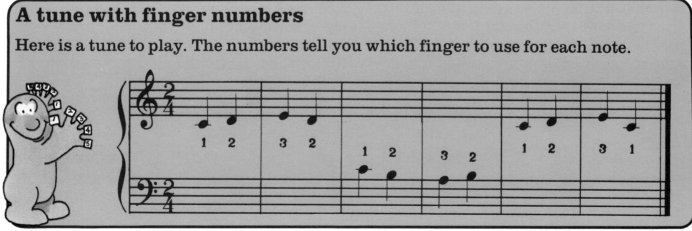

15

More rhythm names

All the tunes you have played so far have been made up of quarter notes. A quarter note lasts for one count only.

Here you can find out about two more notes, called a half note and a whole note. A half note lasts for two counts. A whole note lasts for four counts.

Note symbol	Rhythm name	Counts
o	Whole note	4
♩	Half note	2

1 whole note = 4 counts

2 half notes = 4 counts

4 quarter notes = 4 counts

A whole note is like a whole cake. Each candle on the cake stands for one count.

If you cut the cake in half, each half is like a half note which lasts for two counts.

If you cut the cake into quarters each quarter is like a quarter note. Quarter notes last for one count each.

Clapping and counting – whole and half notes

Try clapping these rhythms which use the two new notes. Clap once for each note. When you clap a whole note, it has four counts to each clap. A half note has two counts to each clap. Count a steady four before you start.

o
(clap) 2 3 4
One clap, four counts.

♩ ♩
(clap) 2 (clap) 4
One clap, two counts.

♩ ♩
(clap) 2 (clap) 4

o
(clap) 2 3 4

Below is a tune for your right hand. It uses the same rhythm which you have just clapped. Remember to count four counts for each whole note and two counts for each half note. The tune starts on Middle C.

Don't forget to count four first.

Hold this note down for a full four counts.

16

Another rhythm

Here is another rhythm to clap. This rhythm starts with a half note.

Underneath it is a tune for your left hand which uses the rhythm.

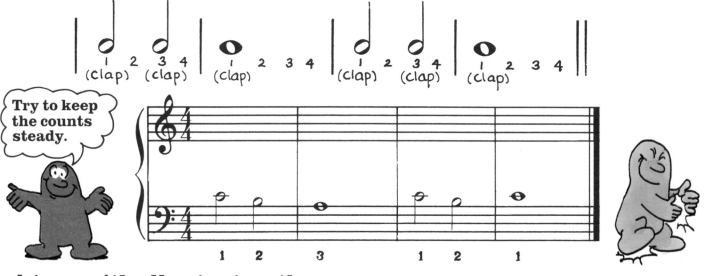

Try to keep the counts steady.

A tune with all notes together

Here is a tune using all the note shapes you have met so far — quarter, half and whole notes. Clap through the rhythm before you start to play.

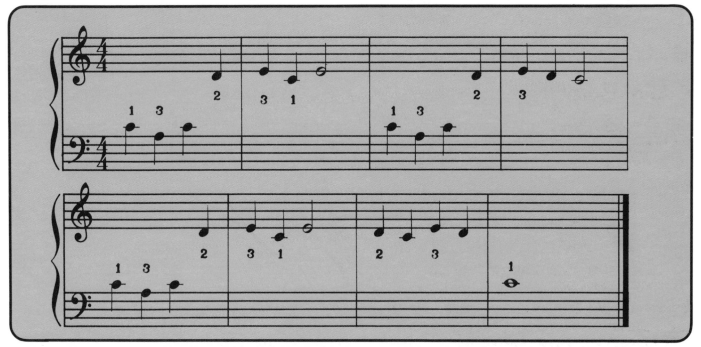

Piano fact

In a grand piano (see page 5) the strings are stretched tightly across a huge iron frame. The force of all the strings pulling on the frame is about equal to hanging a 16 ton weight from it.

Tunes to play

The Swallow's Goodbye

Desert Drums

The Circus Comes to Town

A Windy Day

Silent counts

Some lines of music have gaps in them where no notes are played. Symbols, called rests, in the music tell you how long the gap lasts. A rest lasts for a number of counts, just like a note. You can find out what rests look like below.

Types of rest

The sign on this staff is called a quarter rest. It means that you leave a gap of one count in the music.

This is a half rest. Like a half note, it is worth two counts. You leave a two-count gap in the music.

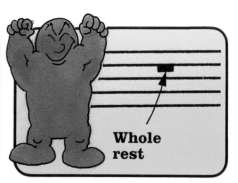

This is a whole rest. It is worth four counts. You leave a gap of four counts in the music.

Each rest is called after the note shape with the same number of counts. For instance, a quarter note and a quarter rest both last for one count.

Counting rests

Clap and count the following rhythm.

When you see a rest, count the rest but don't clap.

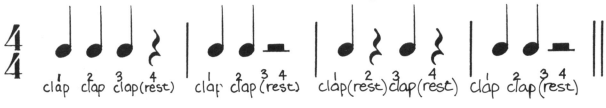

Remembering rests

Note shape	Rest shape	Counts
o	−	4
♩	−	2
♪	𝄽	1

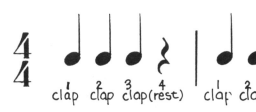

Whole rest

Half rest

Here is a chart to help you remember how many counts each rest has and what they look like.

This rest hangs from the line. Imagine it as a strong rest which can hang on for four counts.

Imagine this rest as a weak rest which has to sit on the line. It only lasts for two counts.

20

A tune with rests

Here is a tune with rests for you to play. Before you play it, clap through the rhythm, leaving a gap when you see a rest.

New notes G and F

Here are two new notes to add to those which you have been using.

A tune for you to play

A whole rest is also used to show a whole bar rest, whatever the time signature.

Tunes to play

Au clair de la lune

French

March Tune

Far, Far Away

Long notes

On this page you will find out about a note shape that lasts for three counts.

On the next page you can see how to join notes together to make a longer sound.

A three-count note

A dot after a note makes the note half as long again. A half note lasts for two counts. A dot adds one count to its length. It becomes a dotted half note.

A half note lasts for two counts.

Half of the length of a half note is one count.

A dotted half note lasts for three counts.

2 counts   +   1 count   =   3 counts

Quiz

Can you work out how long this note lasts for?*

A three-count rest

A three-count rest is written with a half rest (two counts) followed by a quarter rest (one count).

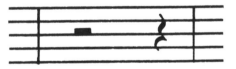

A tune with dotted half notes

Here is a short tune for you to play which uses dotted half notes. Make sure that you hold down each dotted half note for three full counts.

Tying notes together

A note can be made longer by joining it to another on the same line or space with a curved line called a tie. The new note lasts for the same number of counts as the two separate ones added together.

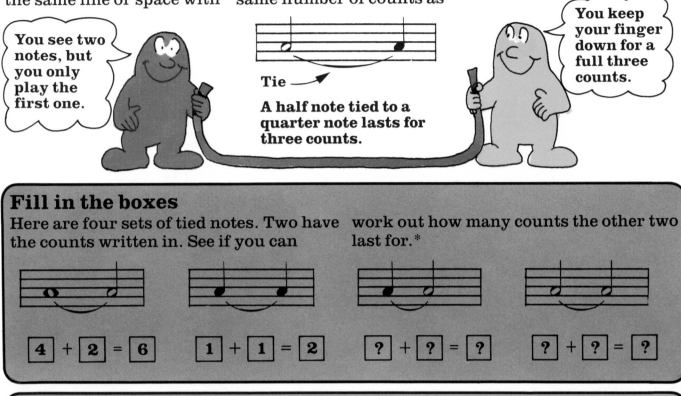

You see two notes, but you only play the first one.

Tie →

A half note tied to a quarter note lasts for three counts.

You keep your finger down for a full three counts.

Fill in the boxes

Here are four sets of tied notes. Two have the counts written in. See if you can work out how many counts the other two last for.*

$$4 + 2 = 6 \qquad 1 + 1 = 2 \qquad ? + ? = ? \qquad ? + ? = ?$$

A tune with tied notes

A tied note can cross a bar line. Before you play this tune, find all the tied notes and work out how many counts each is worth.

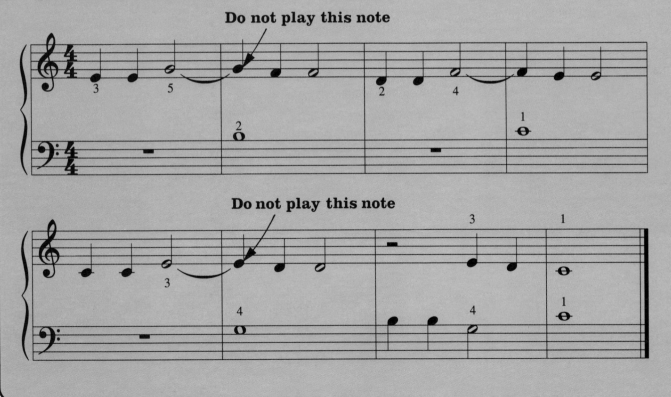

Do not play this note

Do not play this note

Tunes to play

Egyptian Dance

Go and tell Aunt Rhody   **American**

Yankee Doodle

Slow Waltz

Short notes

On these two pages you can find out about some notes that are shorter than quarter notes. These notes are called eighth and sixteenth notes.

Eighth notes

An eighth note is a note that lasts for half a count.

Eighth note →

There are eight eighth notes in a whole note.

There are four eighth notes in a half note.

There are two eighths in a quarter note.

Remembering note lengths

Here is a chart to help you remember how many counts each note is worth. Each line of notes equals four counts.

Whole note = 4 counts
Half note = 2 counts
Quarter note = 1 count
Eighth note = ½ count

Think of cutting a cake into eight pieces. It is like dividing a whole note into eight notes.

Joining eighths

In a line of music, groups of two or more eighths have their stems joined together, like this:

Clapping and counting eighth notes

When clapping or playing eighths it is helpful to say "and" for each note after the count. Try clapping and counting these rhythms.

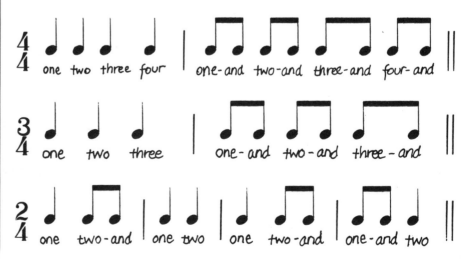

Sixteenth notes

A sixteenth looks like an eighth with an extra tail. It lasts a quarter of a count.

Two sixteenths are the same length as one eighth.

Like eighths, you often see sixteenths in groups.

Sixteenth note

Tails joined.

Clapping and counting sixteenths

There are four sixteenths in one count. You can count a group of four sixteenths as

"one-a-and-a". Look at the examples below to see how this works.

Hint

One sixteenth note equals half an eighth note.

Four sixteenth notes equal one quarter note.

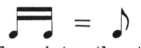

There are 16 sixteenth notes in a whole note.

A tune to play

Here is a tune for you to play. Try not to rush the eighths and sixteenths.

Just keep counting steadily.

Tunes with eighth notes

On this page are two tunes that use eighth notes. Before you play, count through each tune and work out their rhythms.

Starting with part of a bar

Sometimes a tune starts with part of a bar. When this happens, the last bar of the tune contains the remaining counts.

Because the first tune below starts on the fourth count, there are only three counts in the final bar.

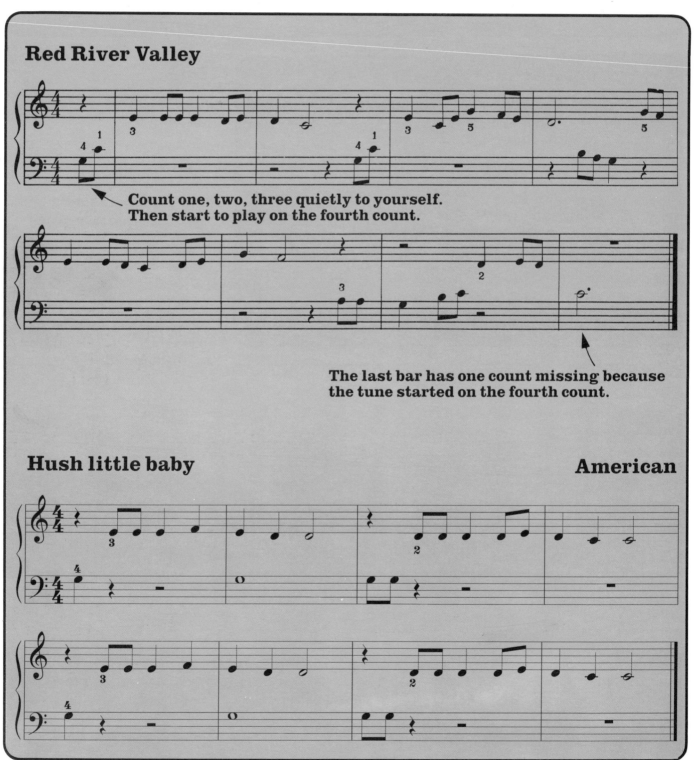

Red River Valley

Count one, two, three quietly to yourself.
Then start to play on the fourth count.

The last bar has one count missing because the tune started on the fourth count.

Hush little baby

American

Dotted quarter notes

You can make a note half as long again by adding a dot to it. A half note with a dot is three counts long (see pages 24-25). A dotted quarter is one and a half counts long.

Half of a quarter is an eighth.

The dot adds an eighth to the length of the quarter.

Try clapping and counting the rhythm below. The dotted quarter is followed by an eighth. Clap the eighth on the "and" of the second count.

one   two   three four | one two-and three four ‖

Do not clap on the "two" count in the second bar. The dotted quarter is one and a half counts long.

A tune to play

Here is a tune for you to play that uses dotted quarter notes.

Slow Song

Black notes

So far, you have been using only the white notes on the keyboard. On the next four pages, you can find out about the black notes.

Sharps

Sometimes in music you will see a sign that looks like the one on the right written before a note.

This is called a sharp sign.

The sign means that instead of playing the note that is written after it on the staff, you play the black note above it on the keyboard.

This is the nearest note above F. It is called F sharp.

A sharp sign is always on the same line or space as the note written after it on the staff.

F sharp is the bottom note in any group of three black notes.

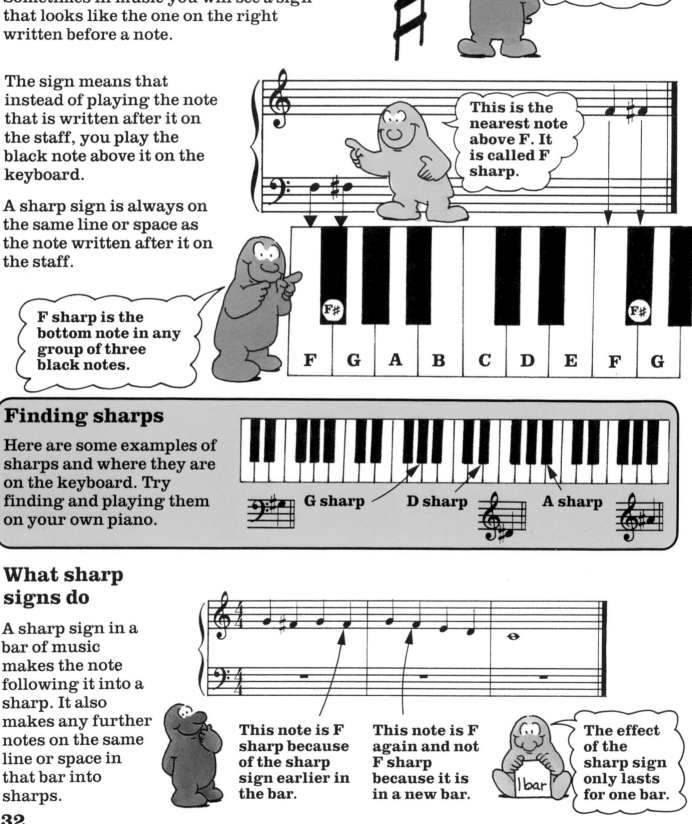

F♯ F♯

F G A B C D E F G

Finding sharps

Here are some examples of sharps and where they are on the keyboard. Try finding and playing them on your own piano.

G sharp   D sharp   A sharp

What sharp signs do

A sharp sign in a bar of music makes the note following it into a sharp. It also makes any further notes on the same line or space in that bar into sharps.

This note is F sharp because of the sharp sign earlier in the bar.

This note is F again and not F sharp because it is in a new bar.

The effect of the sharp sign only lasts for one bar.

1 bar

Key signatures

Some tunes have sharp signs at the beginning just after the clef symbols. The sharp signs tell you what notes in the tune must all be played sharp.

These sharp signs are called the key signature of the music.

This key signature tells you to play F sharp instead of F all the way through the tune, in both clefs.

Key signature

A tune with sharps

Try playing the following tune. Watch out for the sharps.

The F sharp in the key signature makes all the Fs into F sharps in both clefs.

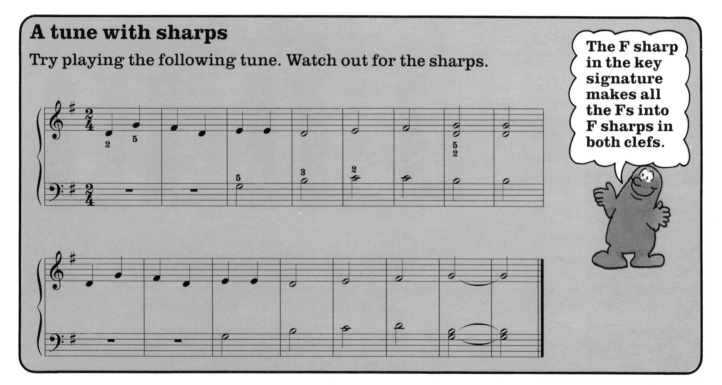

Piano fact

The biggest grand piano ever made weighed 1.43 tons and was 11.6 feet long. It was made in London in 1935.

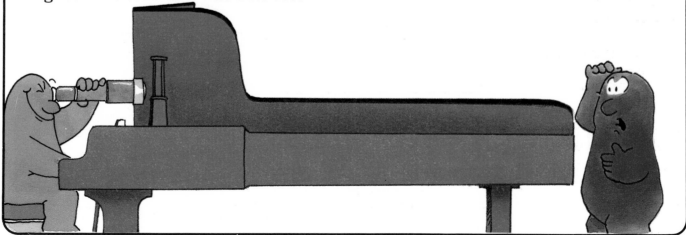

More black notes

As well as being called sharps, black notes on the piano are sometimes called flats. Here, you can find out the difference between sharps and flats.

Flats

This sign is called a flat sign. When you see it in front of a note, you play the black note below the note written on the staff.

Flat signs fit into the lines and spaces on a staff just like notes. A flat sign is always on the same line or space as the note following it.

This is the nearest note below B. It is called B flat.

B flat is the top note in any group of three black notes.

MIDDLE

A B C D E F G A B

Finding other flats

Try to find and play the following flats on the keyboard of your piano.

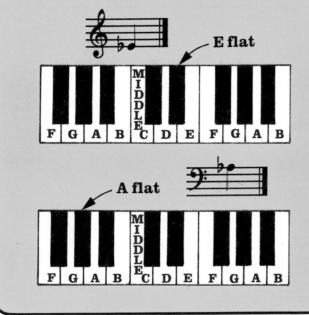

E flat

F G A B **MIDDLE** C D E F G A B

A flat

F G A B **MIDDLE** C D E F G A B

What flat signs do

A flat sign has a similar effect to a sharp sign (see page 32). It lowers a note instead of raising it, though.

The flat sign only applies to this bar.

This note is B flat.

This note is white note B.

Key signatures

Like sharps, flats written at the start of a tune are called a key signature. The flats in the key signature show which notes are flat all through the tune.

Here is a tune with a B flat key signature.

This note is B flat.

Flats and sharps

A black note can be called sharp after the note just below it. It can also be called flat after the note just above it.

A sharp. ——— B flat.

C D E F G A B C

Natural signs

The sign on the right is called a natural. It is written in front of a note on the staff.

Natural

A natural sign cancels the effect of a sharp or a flat sign earlier in the bar or in a key signature.

This note is F sharp because of the key signature.

This note is F because of the natural sign.

The flat sign makes this note B flat.

This is B again.

Accidental roundup

An accidental is a flat, sharp or natural sign in a bar of music.

A sharp raises a note. #

A flat lowers a note. ♭

A natural changes a note from a sharp or flat into a white note. ♮

A tune to play

35

Scales and keys

A black note can be either a sharp or a flat. To find out why, you need to know a bit about scales and keys. Here you can see how to play some scales.

A scale with white notes

Thumb under finger three here.

Finger three over thumb here.

A scale is a set of notes that moves up or down the alphabet. Try playing the eight notes from Middle C to the C above.

Play the notes up and down, following the fingering marked above. This is the scale of C major.

You can start the scale of C major on any C on the piano. Use only the white notes.

A scale with one flat

Now play the notes in the octave from the F above Middle C to the F above that, using only the white notes.

One of the notes in this scale sounds wrong. Can you work out which one it is? Compare it with the scale of C major.

Try the scale again, but play B flat instead of the white note B. This time it sounds right. It is the scale of F major.

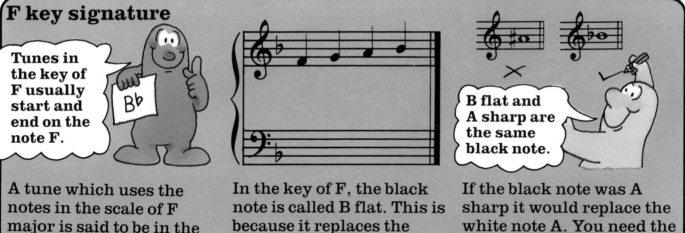

F key signature

Tunes in the key of F usually start and end on the note F.

Bb

A tune which uses the notes in the scale of F major is said to be in the key of F. The key signature is B flat.

In the key of F, the black note is called B flat. This is because it replaces the white note B in the scale of F major.

B flat and A sharp are the same black note.

If the black note was A sharp it would replace the white note A. You need the A in the scale but you don't need B.

A scale with one sharp

Now try building a scale on the note G below Middle C. If you use only the white notes, the scale will sound wrong.

A tune in the key of G

Tunes to play

Slow Tune

Song of the Volga Boatmen

Russian

Lightly Row

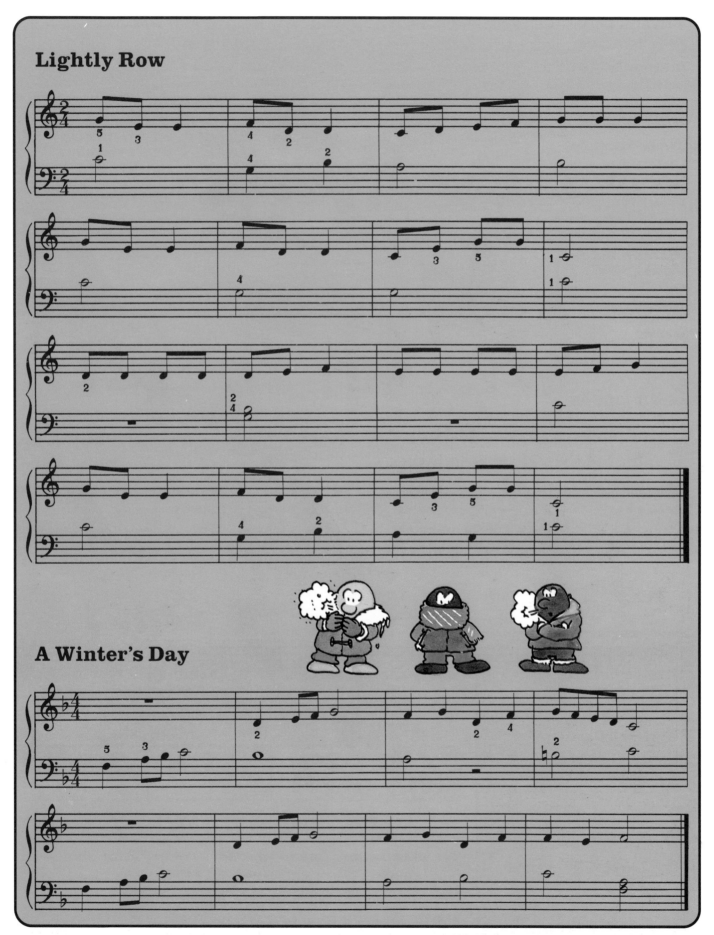

A Winter's Day

Playing loudly and softly

You can play tunes loudly, or softly, or in between. Some tunes have instructions in the music which tell you how loud or soft to play. The instructions are in Italian. Here you can find out what the words mean.

Soft words

There are three instructions which tell you how soft to play. They mean very soft, soft and fairly soft.

The Italian word for soft is *piano*. Press the keys lightly.

Pianissimo means very soft. The ending "*issimo*" means "very".

Piano means soft.

Mezzo (metso) *piano* means fairly soft.

Loud words

The words for loudness in music are based on the Italian word *forte* (for-tay), meaning loud or strong. *Forte* is the second half of the piano's full name. When you play *forte*, press down quickly and firmly.

Fortissimo means very loud.

Forte means loud.

Mezzo forte means fairly loud.

Why are the instructions Italian?

Music printing began in Italy. Italian composers wrote the instructions for how to play their music in Italian. It then became the fashion in other countries to write instructions in Italian.

Instructions in the music

The words for soft and loud are written in the music between the two staffs. Each instruction is shortened to one or two letters.

pp	*p*	*mp*	*mf*	*f*	*ff*
pianissimo	piano	mezzo piano	mezzo forte	forte	fortissimo

Try playing the six notes above, making each one a little louder than the one just before it.

Some tunes to play

Ragtime Capers

River Song

How fast to play

The speed of a tune is called its *tempo*. Most tunes have an instruction in Italian or English at the beginning telling you how fast or slow to play. You can find out about the Italian words for *tempo* on this page.

Allegro

Allegro means lively or fast. A quick march tune can be played *allegro*.

Lento

Lento means slowly. A sad love song could be played *lento*.

Andante

Andante is between *allegro* and *lento*. It means not too slow – at a walking pace.

Presto

Presto is very quick. The *tarantella* (an Italian dance thought to cure a spider's bite) is played *presto*.

Changing speed

The speed of the music may change during the piece. Here are two more words that you will meet.

Ritardando (ri-tar-dan-doe), or *rit.* for short, means slowing down, just like an airplane slows down as it lands.

Accelerando (ah-chel-er-an-doe), or *accel.* for short, means speeding up, like an airplane taking off.

Returning to tempo

After a *ritardando* section, you may see the words *a tempo* written in the music. These words tell you to return to the *tempo* (speed) that you were playing at before you began to slow down.

rit.   a tempo

42

Tunes to play

The Coventry Carol — **English**

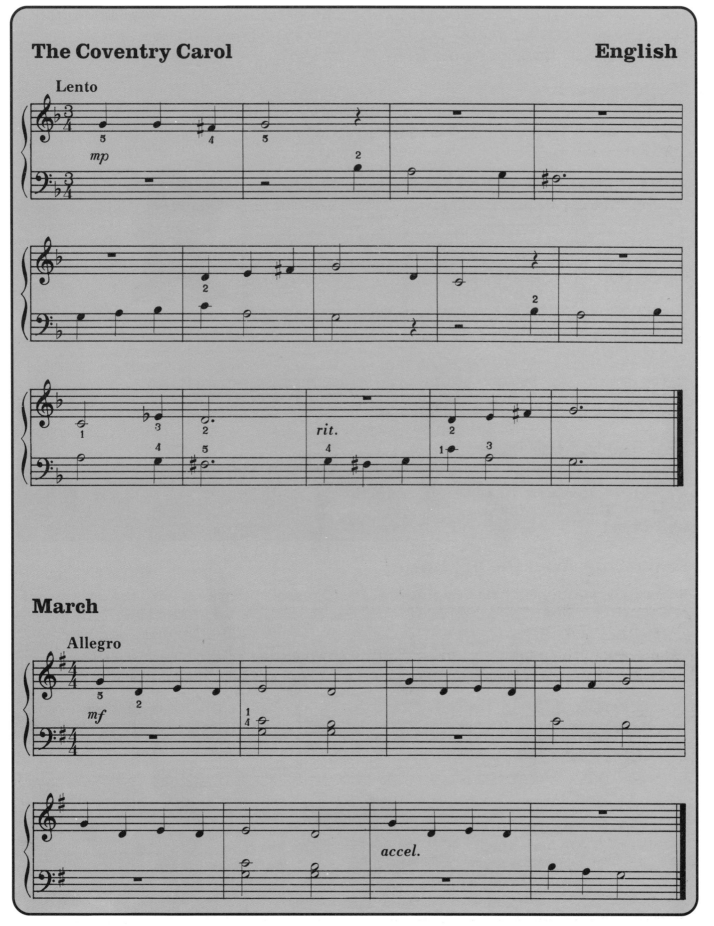

March

Repeats in music

Some tunes contain a section that needs to be repeated. Instead of writing the section out again, there are symbols in the music which tell you to go back and repeat it.

Repeat marks

The marks on the right are repeat marks. They are written on the staff before and after the section of the tune that needs to be repeated.

Repeat marks

How repeat marks work

When you come to the first sign, ignore it and play on.

When you reach the second sign, go back to the first sign and repeat the section.

You only repeat once, or you could go on playing for ever!

When you reach the second sign again, ignore it and play to the end of the tune.

Numbering the bars

If you number the bars above from 1 to 5, this is the order in which you would play them.

| 1 | 2 | 3 | 2 | 3 | 4 | 5 |

Repeating from the beginning

Sometimes you repeat part of a tune from the beginning. In this case there is only one repeat mark, with the dots on the left-hand side.

Start here.

Play the tune to here, then repeat it from the beginning.

After repeating the first part, play to the end of the tune.

This is the order in which you play the bars.

1	2	3
1	2	3
4	5	

44

Quiz

Here are some numbered boxes that stand for bars. See if you can work out the order of the bars using the repeat marks to guide you.*

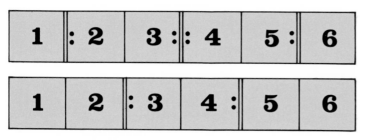

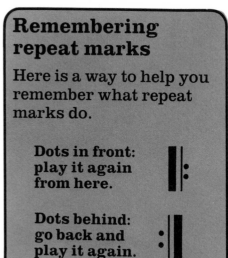

Remembering repeat marks

Here is a way to help you remember what repeat marks do.

Dots in front: play it again from here.

Dots behind: go back and play it again.

Another repeat sign

There is another sign used in music to tell you to repeat a section. This is the instruction *D.C. al Fine.* You may see it at the end of the music.

D.C. al Fine means go back to the beginning and start to repeat the tune. Stop where you see *Fine* written above the staff.

You start here and play to the end of the tune.

You ignore *Fine* the first time.

When you get to *D.C. al Fine*, you play the tune again from the beginning, stopping at *Fine*.

If you number the bars 1 to 6, can you work out what the order is?*

A tune with repeats.

Here is a tune for you to play. Watch out for the repeat marks in the music.

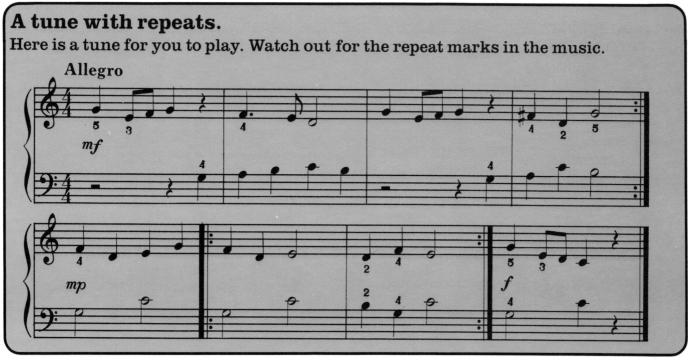

* *Answers on page 63.*

45

First and second time bars

When a tune is repeated, it may have a different ending for the first and second time you play it.

Come to the Fair

Tunes to play

The rest in the last bar of the third line of this tune is an eighth rest.
You leave a gap of half a count in the music.

Ode to Joy

Beethoven

Drink to me only with thine eyes

A new time signature

Here you can find out about a new time signature which uses eighths rather than quarters. You can also learn some new Italian words.

$\frac{6}{8}$ time

Do you remember what the top and bottom numbers in a time signature stand for?

Top number: how many counts in a bar.

Bottom number: what kind of counts.

The six means there are six counts in a bar.

The eight stands for eighth notes.

Count in sixes to keep the rhythm steady.

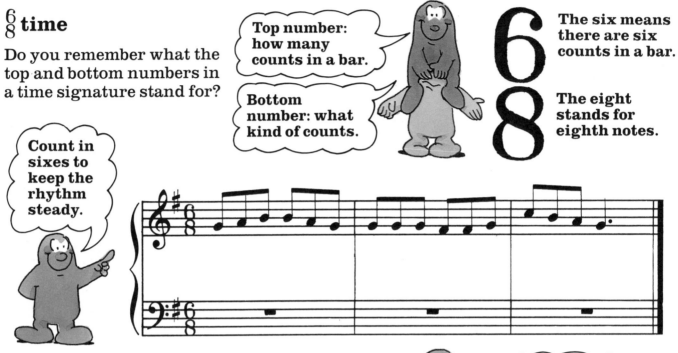

Music in $\frac{6}{8}$ time is often quite fast. To keep the rhythm swinging along, play the first note in each bar a little louder than the rest of the notes.

In $\frac{6}{8}$ time, the eighths are written in two groups of three.

A tune in $\frac{6}{8}$ time

Johnny Murphy's Reel

Irish

Allegro

48

Getting louder and softer

A tune can sound more interesting if the music gets louder or softer within it. Here are the Italian words which tell you when to do this.

Crescendo (cre-shen-doe) means getting louder. The sign for *crescendo* is shown on the right.

This symbol stands for *crescendo*. Sometimes *crescendo* is written *cresc.* for short between the staffs.

To get louder you gradually press the keys down more firmly.

Diminuendo (di-min-u-en-doe) means getting softer. The sign for *diminuendo* is shown on the right.

***Diminuendo* may also be written *dim.* for short between the staffs.**

To get softer you gradually press the keys down more gently.

Remembering the symbols
A way to help you remember what each symbol means is to think of what it looks like.

Crescendo opens out and gets louder.

Diminuendo closes in and gets softer.

An example to try

Crescendo and *diminuendo* do not have to be equal. In this example, you have four counts to get loud but only two counts to get soft again.

Piano fact

The most expensive piano was sold for almost $400,000 at an auction in New York in 1980. It was a Steinway grand piano made in 1888.

Playing staccato

Until now, you have been playing notes very smoothly, with no breaks in between. This is called playing *legato*. The opposite of *legato* is *staccato*. This is to play the notes separately and not joined together.

Legato

To play *legato* you start to press the next note before you have fully taken your finger off the one before. *Legato* can be written between the staffs.

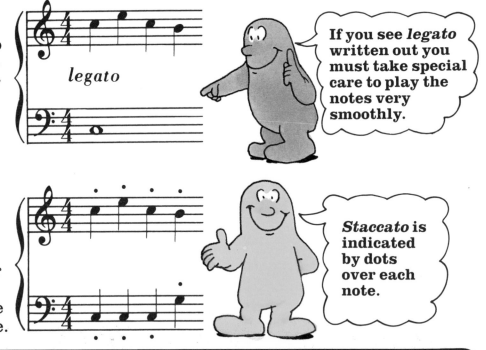

If you see *legato* written out you must take special care to play the notes very smoothly.

Staccato

The opposite of *legato* is *staccato*. Strike the note sharply. Take your finger off as soon as you have pressed it, as if there were rests in between each note.

Staccato is indicated by dots over each note.

Staccato Stomp

Tunes to play

"From the New World" **Dvořák**

Musical sentences

When you want to speak to someone, you organize your thoughts and say them in sentences. In the same way, music has sentences, called phrases.

Phrases

A phrase is a section of a tune. It is made up of a number of bars. A phrase can sound like a short tune in itself.

A phrase is shown by a long curved line written above the music like this.

Play all the notes of the phrase *legato* as if you were singing them in one breath.

This phrase sounds like a little tune by itself. It begins and ends on F.

At the end of a phrase, lift your hand slightly and make a break before you begin the next phrase, as if you were taking a breath.

A long tune usually has several phrases in it.

The lines joining tied notes can look similar to short phrase marks. Remember that a tie joins notes on the same line or space. A phrase mark links notes on different lines and spaces.

When you make sentences you can use questions and answers. It is the same with phrases. The phrase above is like a question.

The tune does not sound complete unless you add this answer phrase. Play the two phrases together to make the complete tune.

Tunes to play

The Brook

Crocodile Waltz

Tunes to play

Lullaby — Brahms

Andante

Kangaroo Hop

This old man

American

She'll be comin' round the mountain

American

Tunes from classical music

Rigadoon

Tunes for two players

On these two pages there are two tunes for you to play with a friend. One person plays part A and the other plays part B at the same time. It will help if you both count one bar together before you begin.

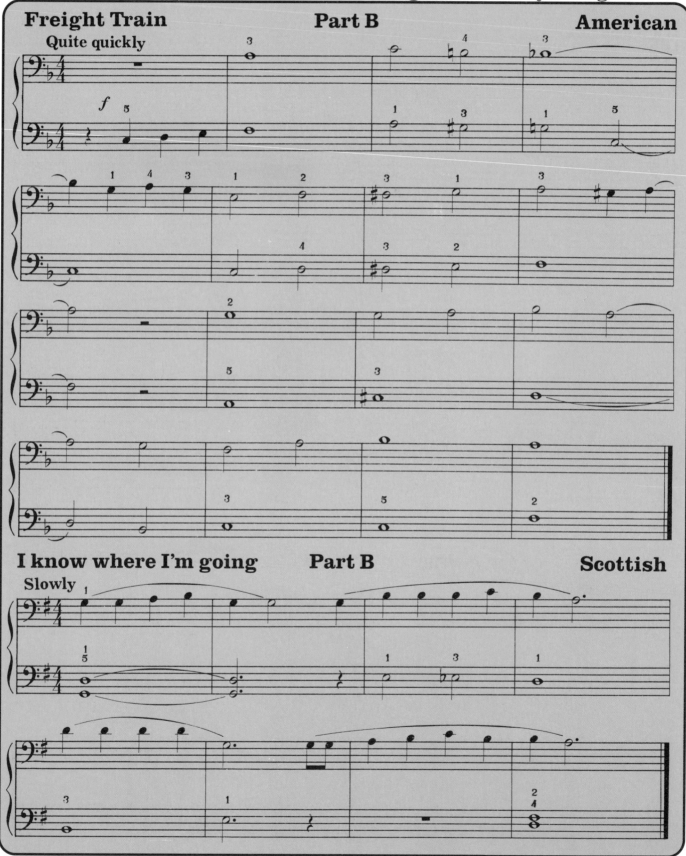

Freight Train   **Part A**   **American**

I know where I'm going   **Part A**   **Scottish**

Christmas carols

While shepherds watched their flocks by night

Traditional

We three kings of Orient are

Traditional

We wish you a merry Christmas

English

Music words

Here you can find explanations for some of the music words used in this book. The list is in alphabetical order. When an explanation includes another music word that is explained elsewhere on these pages, that word is printed in dark type.

Accelerando (accel.) Gradually getting faster.

Accidental Any **natural**, **flat** or **sharp** not part of a **key signature**.

Allegro Fast or lively.

Andante Play "at a walking pace" or not too fast.

A tempo Return to the original speed of the music.

Bar Section of music between two **bar lines**. It contains the number of counts indicated by the **time signature**.

Bar line Upright lines written on the staves dividing the music into **bars**.

Crescendo Getting louder.

D.C. al Fine (short for **Da Capo al Fine**) Go back to the beginning of the tune and play it again, stopping where you see *Fine* written above the staff.

Diminuendo Getting softer.

Dotted note A note followed by a dot. The dot makes the note half as long again.

Duet A tune for two players, with a different part for each.

Eighth note A note that lasts for half a count.

Flat The musical sign that tells you to play the nearest note below the one written on the **staff**.

Forte Loud.

Fortissimo Very loud.

Grand piano A large piano in which the strings are stretched out flat. It is usually used for concerts because it can make a very loud sound.

Half note A note that lasts for two counts.

Key signature **Sharps** or **flats** written at the beginning of a tune, telling you to play certain notes sharp or flat all the way through the tune.

Lento Play slowly.

Legato Play smoothly.

Mezzo forte Fairly loud.

Mezzo piano Fairly soft.

Middle C The note C on the piano keyboard usually nearest to the keyhole of the piano. It is written on its own line between the top and bottom **staffs**.

Natural A sign that tells you to change a note from a **sharp** or a **flat** back into a white note.

Octave The distance (eight notes of a scale) between two notes of the same letter name on the keyboard.

Phrase A section of a tune. Phrases are played *legato* as if you were singing them in one breath.

Pianissimo Very soft.

Piano Soft.

Pitch How high or low a note sounds.